Charles Gayarré

Dr. Bluff in Russia or The Emperor Nicholas

And the American Doctor - A Comedy in Two Acts

Charles Gayarré

Dr. Bluff in Russia or The Emperor Nicholas
And the American Doctor - A Comedy in Two Acts

ISBN/EAN: 9783744767309

Printed in Europe, USA, Canada, Australia, Japan

Cover: Foto ©Andreas Hilbeck / pixelio.de

DR. BLUFF IN RUSSIA.

OR

THE EMPEROR NICHOLAS

AND

The American Doctor.

A COMEDY IN TWO ACTS.

By CHARLES GAYARRÉ.

NEW ORLEANS:
THE "BRONZE PEN" PRINT, 112 GRAVIER STREET.
For sale at the "Bronze Pen" Stationery Store, 62 Bourbon street.

1865.

Dr. Bluff in Russia.

A COMEDY IN TWO ACTS

PERSONAGES:

EMPEROR NICHOLAS.

COUNT NESSELRODE, *Minister of Foreign Relations.*

PRINCE KOURAKIN, *Minister of Justice and of the Interior.*

COUNT PAHLEN, *Minister of War.*

DOCTOR BLUFF, *an American Doctor.*

VISCOUNTESS MORDAUNT, *an English Lady.*

LODOISKA, *Daughter of Nesselrode.*

JAMES, *a Servant of the Viscountess.*

FIRKOFF, *Count Pahlen's Footman.*

retary of War at a moment when Russia needs so much skill and devotion in that department of State, to resist successfully the gigantic struggle she has to maintain against the two greatest powers of the Earth." He then added with a condescending and benignant smile: "This favor, Pahlen, is only a part of the marriage portion which I intend to give you. Choose, without further delay, between the house of Nesselrode and that of Kourakin. It is the policy of a wise sovereign to keep united those great families which are the pillars of the throne." My emotion was so deep, at this sudden announcement of the Imperial pleasure, that I could reply only by a profound bow and by kissing the hand which the Czar extended to me as he passed off. What have we to do now but to wait a while, and seek for a favorable opportunity to extricate ourselves from our difficulties!

VISCOUNTESS.

O heaven! They seem, indeed, to thicken around us.

PAHLEN.

I am distressed beyond expression, dearest. You are so poorly rewarded for the great sacrifices which, for my sake...

VISCOUNTESS.

Do not speak in this desponding mood, Pahlen. I am happy—indeed, I am. Calm your anxieties. You shake your head!—Well, then, I'll tell you a secret. I have hopes, my dear husband, strong hopes, although I did not want to communicate them to you, before there was a probability of their being realized.

PAHLEN.

Indeed! What are they?

VISCOUNTESS.

When my sister, Lady Seymour, departed from St. Petersburg, I wrote through her to my uncle, the Duke of Devonshire. The Duke, you know, resided many years at St. Petersburg as England's envoy, and the Emperor openly professes for him a great deal of esteem, and even of friendship. I explained our position to him, and begged him to put his influence to the test with his imperial friend, and to intercede in our behalf. He immediately answered me that he would do so.

PAHLEN.

How glad I am to hear this! It removes a mountain load off my mind.

VISCOUNTESS.

My uncle further informs me that, as many Americans were coming to Russia in consequence of this war, some from curiosity, and others to offer their services, particularly engineers, doctors, and surgeons, he would seek among them a man of proper qualifications, and intrust him with a letter for the Emperor with secret instructions how to act in the matter.

PAHLEN.

Yes—yes—I see through it. It is very ingenious.

VISCOUNTESS.

It is a good idea; for neither Nesselrode nor Kourakin will suspect such a personage of interfering with their ambitious views, and, through that secret channel of communication, my uncle, the Duke, will have a safe opportunity to make an appeal to the Emperor's generosity, and to his kind remembrance of him. The Emperor, I hope, notwithstanding his habitual sterness of disposition, will.....

PAHLEN.

Thank God—for the proffered relief! There never was a more timely one; for, the cares of State which now assail our august master seem to have rendered him still more unyielding than usual. Nay... since the beginning of this war, signs of irritation are frequent in him—so that I dare not tempt his anger.

VISCOUNTESS.

Let us hope, Pahlen—let us hope. I expect every moment, my uncle's messenger. But who comes?

SCENE II.—ENTER JAMES.

JAMES.

A card for your ladyship.

PAHLEN.

What can it be?

VISCOUNTESS — [*Glancing at the card, and then handing it to the Count.*]

Judge for yourself.

PAHLEN — [*Reading:*]

"Doctor Bluff, formerly from the United States of America, and recently from London, begs leave to visit the magnificent premises occupied by Viscountess Mordaunt, and claims her indulgence for the curiosity of a stranger and a tourist."

VISCOUNTESS.

It must be he, Pahlen. It must be the man alluded to by my uncle, and who takes this means to approach me. I will invite him to come in.

PAHLEN.

It may not be proper that he should see me before you ascertain if your suppositions are correct. I shall make room for him, and shall wait in the next saloon for the result of you interview. [*He walks towards one of the lateral doors.*]

JAMES.

Not in that direction, your Excellency. Count Nesselrode and his daughter have just entered that room.

PAHLEN—[*Astonished.*]

What! Count Nesselrode and his daughter!

VISCOUNTESS.

Yes—I expected them this morning—although not so early. Loiska wrote to me, last evening, that her father, my next neighbor you know, being compelled to return to St. Petersburg, she would accompany him thus far and pass the day with me.

PAHLEN.

Then I shall make my escape through the park. Farewell, love

VISCOUNTESS.

Shall I see you this evening?

PAHLEN—[*Kissing her hand.*]

Sooner if I can. [*Exit.*]

VISCOUNTESS—[*To James.*]

Tell Doctor Bluff that he is welcome to visit the premises, and that, should he have any particular reason to see me, I shall be happy to receive him. Do you understand?

JAMES.

Yes, your ladyship.

VISCOUNTESS.

Then look to it.

JAMES.

Yes, milady. [*Moves away.*]

VISCOUNTESS.

James!

JAMES.

Madam.

VISCOUNTESS.

Now introduce Count Nesselrode and his daughter.

SCENE III.

JAMES—[*Throwing open one of the lateral doors:*]

His Excellency, Count Nesselrodé, and her Ladyship, miss Nesselrode.

VISCOUNTESS.

How happy I am to see you, Count! Dear Lodoiska, how grateful I am to you for this kind visit! Although we are neighbors, you have not, of late, familiarized me too much with such favors. After all, Count, great men who, like you, wield the destinies of empires, have very little time to throw at the feet of such frivolous beings as we are.

NESSELRODE.

Ah! Viscountess—in your presence, even an old statesman like myself would soon forget the destinies of empires.

VISCOUNTESS.

Take care, Count. Don't turn traitor to your country; for you are getting to be decidedly French. This compliment is the proof of it. But I am not the dupe of your politeness. [*To Lodoiska.*] It is to you, dear, that I am indebted for your father's visit, and I should be still more indebted to you, if, instead of a day, you were to pass a week with me.

NESSELRODE.

You have anticipated my wishes. I was going to ask it as a favor. The health of this dear child is not good of late, and I desire for her the benefit of country air. For that purpose, I had intended to rusticate with her a few days; but hardly have I reached my villa, when a sudden order from the Emperor summons me back to St. Petersburg, and God only knows how long I shall be detained there.

VISCOUNTESS.

This, Count, makes amends for your former neglect, and I forgive you.

NESSELRODE.

Then peace is signed between us, and I leave Lodoiska as a hostage with your ladyship. I hope to find her, on my return, more cheerful, and... [*Addressing his daughter*] shall I say more reasonable, my dear?

LODOISKA.

More reasonable! Why—pa—if Lady Mordaunt knew what we disagree about, I am sure she would side with me.

VISCOUNTESS.

What is it, my dear?

NESSELRODE.

Hush!—daughter—hush!—none of your nonsense here.

LODOISKA.

Pshaw!—You know that I am a petted and a spoiled child, father. You say so yourself. Nay—don't shake your finger at me. You may frighten the English and the French, but you won't frighten me.

NESSELRODE.

If you talk so, you shall not have that necklace which.....

LODOISKA.

I'll have it, pa,—talk or no talk. [*Leaning coaxingly on his shoulder.*] Are you not a dear pa—and am I not your beloved?

NESSELRODE—[*Fondly.*]

Yes—my beloved! That you know but too well. But don't be unreasonable—don't.

LODOISKA.

I, unreasonable! It is you who are unreasonable. *You* ought to be ashamed of yourself, to be so unreasonable, and yet to be the Prime Minister of all the Russias! [*Pouting.*] I wonder the Emperor trusts you at all. [*To the Viscountess, returning from the glass doors opening on the park in the back part of the stage, whither she had gone, during the colloquy between Nesselrode and daughter, as if she looked for somebody to make his appearance in that direction, probably the expected Dr. Bluff.*] Do you know what he wants me to do? He wants me to marry a man I don't love! I am sure such a thing would not be thought of in a free country—in England, for instance.

VISCOUNTESS.

I am glad that you have so good an opinion of my country.

NESSELRODE.

What better match can you hope for than Count Pahlen—the Czar's favorite? Besides, he loves you.

VISCOUNTESS—[*Alarmed.*]

[*To Lodoiska :*]—He loves you!

LODOISKA.

No!—he don't.—I know better.—Trust me for that.

VISCOUNTESS—[*Aside.*]

I breathe freely. What a charming child!

LODOISKA—[*To the Viscountess :*]

You know Count Pahlen. Is he not odious?

NESSELRODE.

Well! I am glad of this appeal to your ladyship. Is not, madam, Count Pahlen an accomplished gentleman? Could a father make a better choice for his daughter?

VISCOUNTESS—[*Slightly confused.*]

The Count is rich—a Minister of State—and the descendant of an old and powerful race....

LODOISKA—[*Petulantly.*]

What's that to me?

VISCOUNTESS.

He is handsome.

LODOISKA.

No.

VISCOUNTESS.

Witty.

LODOISKA.

No, no.

VISCOUNTESS.

He is reported to be as brave as he is kind-hearted.

LODOISKA—[*Stamping her foot with girlish impatience.*]

No... no... no.—It is Lipinski who is handsome, witty, and as brave as he is kind-hearted.

VISCOUNTESS—[*Aside.*]

I adore this amiable child. Decidedly she is very pretty. It had not struck me so before.

NESSELRODE.

You hear her, madam! you hear her! You know Lipinski—a hare-brained fellow—tainted with the new-fangled notions of the day—a Pole! whom the Emperor does not like!

LODOISKA.

I love him, if the Emperor don't. I will say so to the Emperor himself. Why should I not speak my mind to him? Is he not my god-father? and has he not bid me never to be afraid of him? [*Aside.*] I am, though—and terribly too.

NESSELRODE.

Madam, I claim your indulgence for the follies of this child.

VISCOUNTESS.

But, really, Count, I do not think her so very unreasonable!

NESSELRODE.

What, madam!—not unreasonable! Consider that Pahlen, young as he is, is the favorite, not only of the Emperor, but also of the heir apparent; consider that the present and the future belong to him; that if he does not marry Lodoiska, he is bound to unite himself to the daughter of Prince Kourakin, my old rival in the confidence of the Emperor. I cannot permit such a thing—it is impossible: reasons of State forbid it.

VISCOUNTESS.

But if Count Pahlen, owing to some unaccountable deficiency of taste, should not be disposed to marry either of those two charming women?

NESSELRODE.

Impossible!—He is too faithful a subject to render himself guilty of such a want of respect for the Emperor. It would be little short of high treason. No, no—when the Czar commands, a Pahlen obeys—or...

VISCOUNTESS—[*Aside.*]

This is dreadful. Heaven protect us!

SCENE IV.—ENTER JAMES.

JAMES.

Doctor Bluff begs leave to present his respects to her ladyship.

VISCOUNTESS.

Show him in.

NESSELRODE.

Dr. Bluff! Where did I see that name? Certainly, something has called my attention to it.

VISCOUNTESS—[*With some show of uneasiness.*]

Do you know any thing of the Doctor?

NESSELRODE.

I think I do, madam. [*Aside.*] Let me see... let me see... Where did I see that name? Ah!... I have it.

VISCOUNTESS—[*Whose uneasiness increases.*]

Do you know the object of his coming here?

NESSELRODE.

No, not exactly. [*Aside.*] I think I do, though. [*Drawing a newspaper from his pocket, he glances at it hurriedly, and says to himself:*] There it is. Lucky it is that this paragraph in the *London Times* struck me.

SCENE V.—RE-ENTER JAMES.

JAMES—[*Opening one of the lateral doors and announcing:*]

Doctor Bluff.

DOCTOR BLUFF—[*With emphasis.*]

I avail myself, madam, of your permission to pay my respects to your ladyship, and I am happy to return you my thanks for the opportunity you have afforded me to admire so many prodigies of art. Truly... this is what I call a princely residence; my admiration increases as I progress, and now [*looking meaningly at the Viscountess*] it has reached its climax. [*Aside.*] That's a hit, I believe. I'll teach these aristocratic folks that we, Americans, are not deficient in high falutin politeness.

VISCOUNTESS.

I am glad, sir, that I have the opportunity of being agreeable to you. [*Pointing to Nesselrode and Lodoiska.*] This is His Excellency Count Nesselrode, and his daughter.

DOCTOR BLUFF.

Sir, I am proud of this introduction to the great minister of a great prince. [*Aside.*] This is another hit. [*To Lodoiska.*] And I am happy to lay my homage at the feet of the sweetest flower in the parterre of all the Russias. [*Aside.*] This is what I call a clincher.

LODOISKA—[*Raising her eye-glass, and surveying him.*]

An amusing original!

NESSELRODE—[*Aside.*]

The fellow does not imagine that I suspect his mission. He is acting an assumed part, the better to conceal the real one.

VISCOUNTESS.

I see from your card that you are recently from England?

DOCTOR BLUFF.

As you say, madam—just the time necessary to run through France, Germany, Poland—and here I am—on my way to St. Petersburg, when, being struck with the appearance of this residence, I begged the favor of being permitted to visit it.

LODOISKA—[*Archly.*]

If you kept *running* all the time, you must have seen very little of the countries you passed through, and yet I am told that they are worthy of all the attention of the traveler.

DOCTOR BLUFF.

On my return, I shall visit them leisurely. For the present, I was in haste to reach St. Petersburg, before the expiration of the summer.

NESSELRODE.

And pray, sir, may I know the pressing interest you have in thus hastening to St. Petersburg? Some great commercial operation, or some speculation or other, I suppose? for, you Americans, whatever be your profession, have still something of the merchant or speculator left in you.

DOCTOR BLUFF.

No, sir. I am nothing but a doctor—a doctor of medicine.... to serve your Excellency, and the present company, if needed—a regular graduate in the Philadelphia school of medicine—and a practitioner for the last twenty years in the State of Mississippi.

NESSELRODE.

Perhaps you are coming to offer your services to his Majesty in this war, as many others have done?

LODOISKA.

Pa, since you are going to talk war and politics as usual, I'll look into the newest Parisian fashions, [*pointing to some engravings on a table*], and select the dress you will have to give me for the next Court ball. [*She takes a chair by the table and examines the engravings.*]

DOCTOR BLUFF—[*Looking at Lodoiska.*]

Sweet darling, that! [*Turning to Nesselrode.*] No, sir; I hate all wars. But I confess freely that I have been prevailed upon to accept a trifling mission to the Czar, and as soon as our Minister Plenipotentiary who, I understand, is momentarily absent, returns, I shall solicit through him the favor of an audience.

VISCOUNTESS.

I hope, sir, that your mission, whatever it be, will end successfully. [*Aside.*] He must be the very individual my uncle was to send me. But I will make assurance doubly sure. [*To Dr. Bluff:*] And pray, sir, how did you like England? I hope that you saw some of its society?

DOCTOR BLUFF—[*Pompously.*]

The very best, madam, the very best. [*Aside.*] A little harmless exaggeration!

VISCOUNTESS.

Some of her distinguished men?

DOCTOR BLUFF.

All of them. [*Aside.*] It would not do to say no.

VISCOUNTESS.

Some of her nobility?

DOCTOR BLUFF.

Intimate with many of them. [*Aside.*] There!.... so much for your Paul-Pry curiosity!

VISCOUNTESS.

Will you permit me, Doctor Bluff, to ask you if you ever met my kinsman, the Duke of Devonshire?

DOCTOR BLUFF.

Met him frequently. [*Aside.*] No lie—for I often met him—riding in the Park!

VISCOUNTESS.

So, you know my dear uncle! [*Aside.*] No longer any doubt—it is he.

NESSELRODE—[*Aside.*]

He is acting the part of a plain, blunt man; that's evident. It increases my suspicions as to the importance of his mission.

VISCOUNTESS—[*Meaningly.*]

Doctor, when I saw your profession by your card, the thought struck me to consult you in the absence of my regular physician. For I am not exactly in the condition in which I wish to be.

DR. BLUFF.

My limited experience and my poor ability are at your service, madam. [*Aside*] What an honor! An English Viscountess! I wish my folks knew it at home.

VISCOUNTESS.

I shall shortly see you in private Allow me to retire for a short time, and show my young friend, who has just arrived, [*Pointing to Lodoiska*] her apartment. Count, you will excuse me. [*Exit with Lodoiska.*]

SCENE VI.—NESSELRODE, DR. BLUFF.

NESSELRODE.

Now that we are left to ourselves, I shall be as plain as yourself, Doctor. I cut matters short therefore, and come at once to the point.

DR. BLUFF—[*Aside.*]

Ah! Ah! Has he some ailment too! [*To Nesselrode*:] I am at your service, Sir.

NESSELRODE.

Well then—let us speak frankly—for you know that, in our profession, we are frequently compelled to disguise truth.

DR. BLUFF.

Not in mine, I assure you. I always speak out bluntly. I disguise nothing—even with my patients. Try me when you please.

NESSELRODE.

Pshaw! Who talks of patients? You understand, I am sure, what I allude to.

DR. BLUFF.

Tut! Not at all, man—I beg your pardon—*your Excellency*. But I am used to be blunt, you see—so much so that, if I were to meet you more than once, you must not be offended should I greet you with: "how are you, Nesselrode—old fellow; I am glad to see you." To save my soul, I could not help it.—It is my nature.

NESSELRODE.

There!......You betray yourself, my good Sir. You overact the part you have assumed—such manners are not yours—they are not natural—they can't be the manners of any human being. The exaggeration is gross. But as you *pretend* to be plain, I'll be still more plain. Do you know this paper?

DR. BLUFF.

It is the London Times.

NESSELRODE.

Well!—Please to give me your opinion of this paragraph. I take some pride in convincing you that nothing escapes the attention of a Russian Statesman. [*Reading:*]

"We are happy to announce the arrival of the distinguished Doctor Bluff, of Bluffville, Mississippi, who is known to be on terms of intimacy with the President of the United States, and who, it is said, is the bearer of important despatches to the American Minister at St. Petersburg. It is further believed, that he is to convey to the Czar the views of the cabinet of Washington in relation to the Eastern war. The sympathies of the Americans are already secured to the Northern despot, and this last official step taken by their chief magistrate tends perhaps to the formation of an unholy alliance, by which they will sacrifice to their selfish desire of national aggrandizement, the great interests of civilization advocated by France and England."

DR. BLUFF—[*With a burst of laughter.*]

Why—this is the mad work of that foolish fellow, Braincut, who is now cutting all sorts of capers in London. He thought it fun to crack that joke at my expense, and to humbug and alarm John Bull, by procuring, God knows by what means, the insertion of this fanciful paragraph into the Times.

NESSELRODE—[*Taking leisurely a pinch of snuff.*]

Very ingenious, indeed. Very! This is warding off the home thrust with consummate skill. I compliment you; but, surely, you don't expect thus to foil my old diplomatic sagacity.

DR. BLUFF.

My dear Sir, I believe you have got into a chronic habit of seeing diplomacy everywhere, just as the jaundiced man, you know.........

NESSELRODE—[*With a shrug of the shoulders.*]

I presume, doctor, there is no actual incompatibility between medicinal art and diplomacy.

DR. BLUFF.

No.—For, they both deal in drugs—with this difference, though—that the object of the first is to heal—and that of the other, to do the reverse. Excuse me—they say at home I am a little rough—like my name. The fact is, I am not used to Court manners.

NESSELRODE.

Well, Sir, as you please. I understand you then to say, that you have no such mission as is hinted at in this paper.

DR. BLUFF.

Distinctly, no.

NESSELRODE—[*With a slight sneering intonation.*]

Then am I permitted to suppose, that the *trifling* mission which you have admitted to have accepted, and which has brought you so far from your distant country—is that of communicating to us some secret of your professional knowledge, by prosecuting your studies in our imperial hospitals?

DR. BLUFF.

No, Sir, no, Sir. But, since you are so pertinacious, I will tell you the truth, the whole truth, and nothing but the truth, as we say in our courts. Know then that, by patient industry, and by a long practice in the town of Bluffville, I have saved enough to secure an income of $4,000 a year—and so—on a hot day, last spring, I got tired of my patients. So—says I to myself: I'll go to Europe like other folks. Done as soon as resolved—and packed my trunk. Great rumor, Sir—great excitement in the town—patients much alarmed—sorry for it—but must go—and just as I was shaking hands with my friends on board the steamboat for New Orleans, up came a deputation from the "Bluffville Consolidated Association of the Friends of Peace," and they handed me a set of "Resolutions," which they requested me to present on their behalf to the Emperor, as they knew I intended to go as far as St. Petersburg.

NESSELRODE.

And you really accepted this *important*—and shall I say—this *only* mission!

DR. BLUFF.

I did, to be sure—as it would give me the opportunity of seeing the Emperor. A great man, Sir! We think him a great man in America! He is our friend, Sir—the friend of the United States! All our Presidents repeat it in their Annual Messages! And Johnathan always sticks by his friends, Sir! And so—says I to myself: I'll have a little talk with the Emperor any how, and that will be something to brag of, at home.

NESSELRODE—[*Aside.*]

This half civilized barbarian astonishes me. He is impenetrable, and cannot be thrown off his guard. [*To Dr. Bluff.*] Well! Sir,—as your Minister happens to be absent for some days, it will afford me pleasure to introduce you to my august master.

DR. BLUFF—[*Bowing low.*]

I am very much obliged to you, Count, and I accept your kind offer. [*Aside, and rubbing his hands*]. What will our folks say at home, when they hear that Dr. Bluff has approached the Emperor without the assistance of the American Legation!

NESSELRODE.

Then the thing is settled. But it is understood that you have no other mission. I can rely...... on your......your [*hesitating.*]......

DR. BLUFF.

Veracity, Sir. Don't mince the word.

NESSELRODE.

Veracity then—to please you. And you further assure me that you have just arrived, and have made as yet no acquaintance whatever in Russia.

DR. BLUFF.

I pledge my word to that effect.

NESSELRODE.

You also promise that you will rely on me, altogether, for your presentation to the Emperor.

DR. BLUFF.

I do.

NESSELRODE.

And you shall not wait long. [*Aside:*] A cunning dog—that! I must not lose sight of him, and must fish everything out of him before he sees the Emperor. But who comes? Ha! It is a man wearing the livery of count Pahlen.

SCENE VII.—ENTER COUNT PAHLEN'S SERVANT.

SERVANT—[*To Dr. Bluff.*]

Count Pahlen, my master, being informed that Dr. Bluff is paying, this morning, a visit to Viscountess Mordaunt, has ordered me to tell him that he would soon be here, to converse with him on the subject he knows of, and begs him to wait until he comes. [*Bows and exit.*]

NESSELRODE—[*Aside.*]

Ha! Ha! What can be the meaning of all this? A preconcerted interview between this man and Pahlen!

DR. BLUFF—[*Astonished.*]

Count Pahlen wishes to see me!

NESSELRODE—[*Ironically.*]

It seems, Sir, that when you told me you knew no one here, you forgot Count Pahlen. Decidedly—a bad memory!

DR. BLUFF.

Upon my word, Sir; I never knew before that the man was in existence.

NESSELRODE — [*Sternly.*]

Allow me to remind you, Sir, that this is carrying dissimulation too far, even for a diplomatist.

DR. BLUFF.

By the Eternal God...... I swear......

NESSELRODE.

Don't swear...... but cease to dissemble, since you have been thus accidently betrayed; and believe me, the best policy now is to tell me the object of your interview with Count Pahlen.

DR. BLUFF.

How can I guess at it, unless it be that Count Pahlen, being despaired of by the Russian faculty, wants to try an American doctor!

NESSELRODE — [*With much dignity.*]

Sir, I have done with one who acts with such levity. I will only say that I am amazed at the pertinacity with which you continue to affirm, after the message delivered to you in my presence from Count Pahlen, that you had no other object in coming here than the gratification of your curiosity, and the presentation to the Emperor of an insignificant address from a few of your fellow citizens, about matters with which they have nothing to do

DR. BLUFF — [*Exasperated.*]

This is really beyond endurance—you will drive me mad. Well! Sir—since you persecute me so, I will confess, although I might keep it to myself, because it is no concern of yours, and is strictly professional, that I have another object in view.

NESSELRODE — [*Aside.*]

At last!—I knew it would come out.

DR. BLUFF.

You want me to tell you all?

NESSELRODE.

I think it is my duty, as Minister of his imperial majesty, to insist on it.

DR. BLUFF.

Well, then—do you know Swaim's panacea?

NESSELRODE.

What! What!

DR. BLUFF.

It cures everything, Sir, and has made Swaim as rich as Crœsus.

NESSELRODE.

What nonsense is this!

DR. BLUFF.

Nonsense!—Do you know Townsend's sarsaparilla? It so renovates the system, that it would turn an old man like you into a young one—and, what is better, it has put five hundred thousand dollars into Townsend's pocket.

NESSELRODE.

Do you dare thus to trifle with me!

DR. BLUFF.

Trifle!—Wait a little. Do you know Dalley's pain extractor? It will extract every rheumatism out of your bones, and set you a dancing a jig, like any Virginia country belle. It is making the fortune of its inventor.

NESSELRODE.

I cannot listen any longer to such......

DR. BLUFF.

Ah! but you must, though—since you want to know all the secrets of my profession. Know then that I came here with the intention of imitating these good examples, and of putting out in the market, when I return home, another universal remedy—which I shall call Dr. Bluff's Cossack elixir.

NESSELRODE.

Stop, Sir—no more of these fooleries, and listen to words of serious import. You have been detected in a mysterious correspondence with Count Pahlen under suspicious circumstances, made still more so by your denegations. I warn you that I shall give immediate information of it to the Emperor.

DR. BLUFF.

Do what you please, O most acute and incredulous of Ministers! But I affirm that I never saw Count Pahlen, and that I have no business with him whatever.

NESSELRODE.

It seems that *he* has—for I see him coming through the park, no doubt to meet you.

DR. BLUFF.

Is that Count Pahlen?—Well! Let him come. We shall see. [*Aside.*] It seems that I am a more important man than ever I thought, and that some great mission, or other, has been tacked to the tail of my coat without my being aware of it.

SCENE VIII.—NESSELRODE, DR. BLUFF, PAHLEN.

JAMES—[*Announcing:*]

His excellency Count Pahlen.

PAHLEN—[*Aside.*]

Good God!—Nesselrode still here!

NESSELRODE.

Really, Count, this is an unexpected pleasure to meet you here.

PAHLEN.

I was on my way to your excellency's country seat, on some State business, when seeing your equipage in the court-yard of the Viscountess, I entered.

NESSELRODE.

And you did well. [*Aside.*] The Count lies prettily, and does not suspect I know he came for Dr. Bluff.

PAHLEN—[*Feigning to recognize Dr. Bluff.*]

But who have we here? Dr. Bluff—I declare!

NESSELRODE—[*Aside.*]

The surprise is well acted—upon my word, it is very well acted.

PAHLEN.

I am glad to meet you thus accidentally, Doctor. How long have you been in Russia?

NESSELRODE.

Why!—Doctor, I thought I had heard you say you knew no one in Russia. [*To Pahlen.*] Count, the Doctor seems to be an old acquaintance of yours?

PAHLEN.

More than an acquaintance—he is an old friend. I had the advantage of knowing him when I was Minister at the Court of St. James. The Doctor was then on a visit to England—and I happened to be much benefited by his medical advice. Welcome to Russia, Doctor. [*Shakes hands with the Doctor and whispers to him:*] Don't contradict any of my statements. We must blind the old fox. [*The doctor looks much puzzled, and stares alternately at Nesselrode and Pahlen.*]

NESSELRODE—[*With ironical gravity, to Doctor Bluff:*]

Sir, I compliment you on your meeting again so old and so valuable a friend as Count Pahlen. [*Aside.*] The fellow has brass enough in his composition. Although fully exposed, he is still acting, and trying to deceive. [*To Pahlen and Dr. Bluff:*] Let me not interfere with your meeting. Old friends must have so many things to say to each other! I shall occupy myself with reading certain despatches, whilst awaiting the return of the Viscountess. [*Aside:*] I'll keep an eye on them. [*He takes a seat by a table which is at some distance from the Doctor and Pahlen.*]

PAHLEN. [*To the Doctor.*]

That won't do, to allow him to remain in the room. Can't you devise some pretext or other to drive him away? It would come with a better grace from you than from me. Tax your diplomatic skill, and do it.

DOCTOR BLUFF—[*Aside.*]

Here is another with crooked ways and mysteries! [*To Pahlen.*] And so—you want to get rid of the old man?

PAHLEN.

Of course. But it must be done in such a way, that he must not suspect anything.

DR. BLUFF.

Good! He must not suspect anything, hey! [*Aside*] I'll give you secrecy and diplomacy with a vengeance. [*Approaching Nesselrode.*] Sir!.... [*Nesselrode looks up.*] Do you know what that gentleman yonder wants?

NESSELRODE.

No.

DR. BLUFF.

He wants me to find out some pretext or other, to send you out of the way.

NESSELRODE. [*Staring with astonishment.*]

You are bold, Sir—very bold indeed! But I understand.... I leave you master of the field, although I warn you that you will not baffle me long. [*Aside.*] I must seek the Emperor, without loss of time, and inform him of all that is going on. [*Exit.*]

SCENE IX.—PAHLEN, DR. BLUFF.

PAHLEN.

How lucky to have thus got rid of him!—and you had but one word to say! With what exquisite tact you must have managed it!

DR. BLUFF.

Tact, or no tact—you won't be troubled with him any more—I have settled that—and now speak out. [*Aside.*] It is time that I know what all this means.

PAHLEN.

Yes—for I am in a great hurry, and not a minute is to be lost.

DR. BLUFF.

To the point then. [*Aside.*] Bless my stars, when will these people ever come to the point!

PAHLEN.

Well, Doctor, have you seen the Viscountess?

DR. BLUFF.

Yes, Sir.

PAHLEN.

And you are what she expected?

DR. BLUFF—[*Impatiently.*]

So it seems; for she wishes to consult me in private. [*Aside.*]. Some lover, I presume, who takes great interest in the health of the Viscountess.

PAHLEN.

Then, God be praised! I was dying with impatience to know whether you are the right person. Now, I am satisfied. Do all that the Viscountess recommends. I will sanction all; for we fully understand each other. Farewell—I must hasten to St. Petersburg.

DR. BLUFF.

Stop, Sir—this does not explain how it is that......

PAHLEN.

I have no time to spare. The Viscountess will explain all. Only one word more. Call on me to-morrow. I shall obtain an audience for you from the Emperor. Do not, then, hesitate to fulfil at once your mission to him. The crisis must be met boldly and fearlessly. [*The Doctor looks completely bewildered.*] Yes, Sir, there must be no more shrinking. For my part, I am ready to meet the storm, and know at once whether I am to sink, or swim. [*Turns to go away.*]

DR. BLUFF.

Stop—Sir. I insist on your explaining how......

PAHLEN—[*Whose excitement increases.*]

What explanations! I can't remain in such a position any longer. Tell my august master, in the most positive terms, that I can gratify neither Nesselrode, nor Kourakin, and that I cannot agree to either of the alliances they propose, honorable as they are, on account of the previous engagements contracted in another quarter, and which I will not suffer to be broken, or annulled, even by the imperial will—no—were I to be sent to Siberia.

DR. BLUFF.

To Siberia!

PAHLEN.

Ay! To Siberia. That's his way. But show him immediately the paper which you have in your possession and which makes such an appeal to his good feelings. [*Exit.*]

SCENE X.

DR. BLUFF—[*Alone.*]

Paper!... He must mean the address of the "Bluffville Consolidated Peace Association," of which he must have heard. But what can it have to do with the alliances he speaks of?—Oh! I have it. Those alliances must have for their object, either to continue the war, or re-establish peace. Hence the bearing upon them of the address of the "Bluffville Peace Association." But what are those alliances?......One thing is clear—his Majesty's Ministers don't agree about them. The Muscovite Cabinet is not a unit, as we say in Washington. Kourakin is for a certain alliance; Nesselrode for another; and Pahlen for a third. Some deep intrigues are going on, and it is intended that I shall take in them a part which, so far, I am utterly at a loss to comprehend. What a mysterious affair! Will they ever believe it in the United States! But somebody comes. I hope it is the Viscountess, who seems the person destined to give me all the explanations which I need. But no. It is not the Viscountess.

SCENE XI.—ENTER LODOISKA, *Hastily*

LODOISKA.

Where are you, Doctor? I am sent in haste to you by the Viscountess.

DR. BLUFF.

Here I am. What is it?—What is it?

LODOISKA.

Great news!—Great news!—Do you hear all that noise?

DR. BLUFF.

Yes—I do. For God's sake, what is it? You seem so agitated!

LODOISKA.

It is the Emperor.

DR. BLUFF.

The Emperor!

LODOISKA.

Yes—his Imperial Majesty. It so happens that he met on the road to St. Petersburg my father, whom he has ordered to go back, and to accompany him to this place.

DR. BLUFF.

Oh! I see through it—Count Nesselrode has fulfilled his threats. He was to denounce me and Count Pahlen to the Emperor, for some supposed correspondence and secret understanding which he suspects to exist between that gentleman and myself.

LODOISKA.

I know nothing about all that. I come in haste, merely to deliver to you a short message from the Viscountess. Taken by surprise by the Emperor's sudden arrival, she said to me: "Do me the favor to go to the Doctor, who is waiting for me in the drawing-room, and tell him that our interview must be postponed for to-day—that Count Pahlen will give him all the necessary information he wants—and that he can act entirely according to the Count's directions; for we fully understand each other. Now—farewell! I must run off to meet the Emperor in time. [*Runs out.*]

DR. BLUFF—[*Alone.*]

They fully understand each other! But I don't understand anything. I must try to do it, though. I can't continue in this fog. [*Seems to reflect.*] Ha! A flash of light comes upon me. I have it.... I have it. This Viscountess..... must be an English spy..... a secret envoy..... or some such thing. Through her, England, without being suspected by "*Parlez-vous Français,*" proposes terms to Russia. This Count Pahlen accepts them. Nesselrode and Kourakin are against this game; they are for continuing this war as it is, and for strengthening Russia by some other alliances. Ha! My wily court intriguers, plain Doctor Bluff is on your trail, and will track you with the unerring sagacity of a backwoodsman. I'll match you all yet. Bless me! What will they say in the United States, when they hear of all this! I'll publish a full exposé when I go home. What a sensation!....But here comes the whole imperial pageantry.

SCENE XII.—EMPEROR, KOURAKIN, PAHLEN, NESSELRODE, VISCOUNTESS, LODOISKA, DR. BLUFF—SUITE.

EMPEROR—[*To the Viscountess.*]

You see, Madam, that although at war with England, I dare claim her hospitality.

VISCOUNTESS.

England deplores the war, Sire, and cannot but be proud of the great honor done to her by her august guest.

EMPEROR.

Last evening, I sent in haste a despatch to your neighbour, Count Nesselrode, calling him back to St. Petersburg. But, this morning, I reflected that my faithful subject—my old friend—needed some rest. I determined to surprise him by an early ride to his residence, and thus spare him the fatigues of the journey. I met him, however, on the way, and so near your Villa, that I could not resist the temptation to stop, and avail myself of this opportunity to thank you, Madam, for the compliment you pay to Russia, by continuing to reside in her bosom, notwithstanding the untoward events which, momentarily, I hope, divide two nations whose interest it is to remain ever united.

VISCOUNTESS.

Sire, a lasting alliance between Russia and England, is the most fervent wish of my heart. It would secure forever the peace of the world.

DR. BLUFF—[*Aside.*]

There comes the cat out of the bag! I had guessed right. Perfidious Albion is going to drop too confiding France.

EMPEROR—[*With a smile—to the Viscountess.*]

Well! Madam—as I have met, this morning, two of my Ministers, Count Pahlen and Count Nesselrode, coming out of your house, I suppose that there must be between you some secret negotiations going on, which will end in happy results.

VISCOUNTESS.

Those happy results, Sire, may be forwarded by the appeal which is to be made to your generosity and magnanimity by Doctor Bluff, from the United States of America, and whom I beg leave, thus informally, to introduce to the kind notice of your Majesty. Dr. Bluff is recently from England, where he has seen my uncle, the Duke of Devonshire, and I believe that he has some mission near your Majesty.

EMPEROR—[*To Doctor Bluff.*]

I am always glad to see Americans. They are a straightforward and manly people, and their government is worthy of them. I look upon the

United States as my natural allies, and shall be happy, Sir, at the earliest opportunity, to take cognizance of the business you have to lay before me

DR. BLUFF.

Sire—these people around you are laboring under some strange hallucination. I have no other mission than that of laying before your Majesty an address from the "Bluffville Peace Association."

NESSELRODE—[*Aside.*]

With what ability he conceals his purposes, until he developes them to the Emperor in private! A wonderful man, indeed!

EMPEROR—[*To Doctor Bluff.*]

Nothing can be more agreeable to me, Sir, than such a mission as yours. Peace? I think of nothing else, and if my heart were opened, the word *peace*, would be found inscribed in it. [*Aside, to Nesselrode.*] This is the sentiment to be proclaimed, Nesselrode, on all occasions, until we get to Constantinople.

DR. BLUFF.

I must not permit your Majesty to remain under any misapprehension. I am plain Dr. Bluff, and no diplomate; and as to those "Peace Resolutions," your Majesty must not suppose that the President of the United States ever authorized me to....

EMPEROR.

Be at ease, Sir—be at ease. I love plain men. But no explanations are necessary for the present.

DR. BLUFF—[*Aside.*]

He also wants no explanation!.... They are all alike.

EMPEROR.

Let business, Sir, be postponed to a more auspicious moment—although I have here all the materials to hold a Cabinet Council. Here is Nesselrode my Minister of Foreign Affairs, Kourakin the Minister of Justice and of the Interior, and Pahlen the Minister of War. Almost a full council.

LODOISKA.

And with your Majesty's consent, I will act as Secretary to the Council.

EMPEROR.

Ha! My pert god-daughter, I should have been astonished if you had not had something to say! No—no—damsel, I don't accept your services in such serious matters. I reserve you for the department of Court Ball invitations. And this, by the by, puts me in mind that the Empress has a small private re-union this evening. Will she have the pleasure of being favored with your company, Viscountess?

VISCOUNTESS.

Sire, I am deeply grateful for your Majesty's condescension. But, under present circumstances, would it be proper for me to show myself at Court?

EMPEROR.

Am I not at your house, Madam? [*Viscountess bows low.*] Besides, it would only be returning my visit, and this, I believe, would not be an impropriety, even in times of war. Moreover, as I have told your Ladyship, it is a very private re-union. Alas! In these sad times, when so much blood is shed, gaiety is not permitted to enter the house of the Sovereign of Russia.

VISCOUNTESS.

May it soon return to that august abode, Sire, with all its train of pleasures! This is the wish I shall express, to-night, to your Majesty's noble consort.

EMPEROR—[*To Dr. Bluff.*]

Let America, to-night, be represented by you, Doctor. It will afford me pleasure.

VISCOUNTESS.

Allow me, Sire, to lead you to the adjoining room, where some refreshments await your Majesty.

[*The Emperor offers his arm to the Viscountess, and the whole company moves off, save Dr. Bluff.*]

DR. BLUFF—[*Alone.*]

Now, I'll go post haste to St. Petersburg without loss of time, to provide myself with a decent suit of clothes for the occasion. But, certainly, these Russians are the most extraordinary set of people on the face of God's earth. They know a man's secrets—when he has none! They give no explanations when desired, and they accept none when offered!—Upon my word, it produces more confusion than Shakspeare ever put in "Midsummer Night's Dream." But I am not the man to play Bully Bottom, and have an ass's head clapped on my shoulders. No. I'll know, this very evening, before going to bed—what is what—or I'll lose the name of plain Doctor Bluff.

ACT II.

SCENE I.

A room in the Imperial Palace, at St. Petersburg.

ENTER NESSELRODE AND LODOISKA.

LODOISKA.

You have hurried me, father, to come to this soirée—which is unusual with you; for at any Court Ball, or other like entertainment, you are sure to be always the last to make your appearance.

NESSELRODE.

Yes.—I was anxious to be among the first here, with the hope of meeting Doctor Bluff before he speaks to the Emperor.

LODOISKA.

That American Doctor, still in your mind! He must be a very important man, indeed!

NESSELRODE.

An important man he is, or must become, if his other faculties are equal to his brass, and powers of dissimulation. But I am not his dupe. Truly, those Americans are astonishing. They are Jacks at all trades. Here is a physician—a bad one, I dare say—who turns out to be an excellent diplomatist.

LODOISKA.

But, after all, what have you detected in that American Doctor to make you uneasy?

NESSELRODE.

What I have detected! Why!—a host of things.

LODOISKA.

You frighten me, Pa, with your penetration!

NESSELRODE.

In the first place, he has a secret mission from the United States, and he denies it to me! First symptom. He comes post haste to Russia, under the most frivolous pretexts. Second sympton. He is an old acquaintance of Count Pahlen, and is in mysterious correspondence with him about something, or other. That, he denies also. Third symptom and last, where did I first discover that man, who seems to have dropped from the clouds?—Why—at the house of that English Viscountess whom I have long suspected. And there is nothing at the bottom of all this!

LODOISKA.

Suppose there is something. What have you to fear?

NESSELRODE.

What I have to fear?...... The *intimacy* of that infernal American Doctor with Count Pahlen The Emperor attaches a great deal of importance to possessing, in the present struggle, the moral force which he thinks he will derive from the sympathies of the United States. May not that Doctor's mission be of such a nature as to meet the Emperor's views in that respect? And will Pahlen be the *first* to know that mission? Will he be the *first* to communicate it to the Emperor? My credit at Court would greatly suffer from it.... and if, after that, Pahlen were to marry the daughter of my old rival Kourakin, it would be inferred that my star has set, or is setting forever.

LODOISKA.

But here comes this dreaded Doctor, with the borrowed plumage of a peacock. O! how he struts!

SCENE II.—DR. BLUFF, NESSELRODE, LODOISKA.

DR. BLUFF—[*Bowing right and left.*] *To Lodoiska:*

How pretty you look, Miss Nesselrode! I kiss my hand to you. [*Aside.*] That is courtly, I hope. [*To Nesselrode.*] How grand you look with all your crosses and stars! [*Aside.*] Flattery is the drug to be used in this atmosphere. [*To Nesselrode:*] How do you think I look in this costume?

NESSELRODE.

Very natural—I assure you—Sir. Very natural.

DR. BLUFF.

Hem! Hem! I have my doubts about it—you see. We are not used to such flummery at home. But let it pass for once. Where is the Emperor?

NESSELRODE.

In the inner appartments. But, once for all, Sir, before you see him, allow me to put you again in mind that, as Minister of Foreign Affairs, I have the right to be the first to be informed of the object of your mission here.

DR. BLUFF.

Gracious God! Am I again to be pestered with these groundless suppositions? And if I had really any serious business to transact, is this the time and place for it?

NESSELRODE—[*Smiling.*]

As to that, my good Sir, State secrets are as often communicated in the ball room, as anywhere else, and it is not always in the Ministerial Offices that the most important negotiations are conducted and terminated.

LODOISKA.

The fact is, Doctor, that it is time to put an end to my father's uneasiness. Remember the Message which I carried to you, this morning, from the Viscountess. It certainly meant that there are confidential relations existing between you, the Viscountess, and Count Pahlen.

DR. BLUFF.

Heavens! This caps the climax. I shall go distracted. Strange how appearances work!

NESSELRODE.

Ha! Ha! Doctor. Fairly caught—hey?—and by a child! Now what do you say?

DR. BLUFF.

What I say? [*Aside.*] Ah! When I speak the truth to you all, my gentle folks, you don't believe me! Well—I'll serve you according to your taste.

NESSELRODE,

Yes—what do you say?

DR. BLUFF.

I understand you, Count, to be satisfied that I have a secret mission. Hey !.....

NESSELRODE.

I am.

DR. BLUFF

Well, I am satisfied too, if you are. [*Aside.*] I'll humor them all with a vengeance.

NESSELRODE.

This being at last admitted, I suppose that you can have no longer any objection to communicate to me, briefly, the outlines of that mission, so that I may prepare the Emperor to hear it.

DR. BLUFF—[*With an assumed air of offended dignity.*]

I will not tell it to you, Sir. That is precise, and to the point, I believe. [*Aside.*] A very good reason I have for not telling him anything.

NESSELRODE—[*Sternly.*]

That is enough. I shall know how to resent this want of respect. Well!—Sir,—play your game, as you understand it. I shall play mine. Daughter, follow me.

LODOISKA.

Allow me, father, to say a few words to the Doctor.

NESSELRODE—[*Abruptly.*]

No.—[*With a milder tone.*] Yes—as you please. [*Exit.*]

SCENE III.—DR. BLUFF, LODOISKA.

LODOISKA—[*Approaching the Doctor coaxingly.*]

Doctor, my father, seems to think that you are a dangerous man!

DR. BLUFF—[*With an affectation of sterness.*]

I am.

LODOISKA.

A very important man!

DR. BLUFF.

I am very important. [*Aside.*] So, at least you all seem to think.

LODOISKA.

Coming here with very dark purposes!

DR. BLUFF.

Dark—very dark indeed. [*Aside.*] So dark, that I cannot see through them myself.

LODOISKA.

Everybody thinks that you have great influence with Count Pahlen.

DR. BLUFF.

Everybody must be right.

LODOISKA.

Dear Doctor, such being the case, will you do me a great favor?

DR. BLUFF—[*Smiling benignantly.*]

A favor to you, sweet girl! What favor can I refuse you? But speak plain. Don't be like those other folks. Tell me something that I can understand.

LODOISKA.

O yes—something very plain—which you will understand, and Count Pahlen too.

DR. BLUFF.

That is right. Well! What is it?

LODOISKA.

Just tell Count Pahlen that I entreat him to reject, as soon as possible, the alliance desired by my father.

DR. BLUFF.

Ay.—The message is plain enough:...... "that you entreat him to reject the alliance desired by your father."

LODOISKA.

In so many words.

DR. BLUFF.—[*Aside.*]

So young!.... and yet she already deals in politics! Faith! It is not without reason that all the Russian ladies are said to be politicians. [*To Lodoiska.*] But, my beautiful damsel, is it not unnatural thus to side against your father!

LODOISKA.

I can't help it. My happiness depends on the rejection of that alliance by Count Pahlen.

DR. BLUFF.

Does it?... Well then...... I'll make you happy at once by telling you that Count Pahlen, this very morning, has requested me to inform the Emperor, that he could not give his assent to such an alliance.

LODOISKA—[*Clapping her hands.*]

Oh! Indeed! you make me happy, as you say. With your permission, I'll run to tell father all about it—and dear Lipinski too, whom I just met on his way to the Palace, and who looked so dejected. [*Exit.*]

DR. BLUFF.

So—the work goes on bravely! But what kind of work it is—I am not responsible for. That's clear. Now—I'll make my way straight to the Emperor. But here comes Prince Kourakin. I hope he is not going to plague me too, like the rest of them.

SCENE IV.—ENTER PRINCE KOURAKIN.

KOURAKIN.

I have the honor to salute the *secret* Envoy of the United States.

DR. BLUFF—[*Aside.*]

Exactly! The same cap fits them all. [*To Kourakin.*]—My respects to Prince Kourakin.

KOURAKIN.

I have been in search of you to tell you, Sir, that I shall be happy to know from your own lips the views of the Cabinet of Washington, particularly in relation to the pending struggle. Should you repose confidence in me, I will, if it be consistent with my duty, avail myself of the ear of the Emperor to favor your designs.

DR. BLUFF.

I shall be grateful, Sir, for anything you may deem proper to do for me. [*Aside.*] Here is another, fishing for pretended secrets existing only in his brains!

KOURAKIN—[*Pointing to seats.*]

Pray, Sir, let us be seated. [*Aside, with exultation.*] He is going to open himself to me, when that cunning old fox, Nesselrode, could not get anything out of him. What a triumph! [*They take seats, and look at each other in silence, and as if each one expected a communication from the other.*]

KOURAKIN—[*Getting impatient.*]

I thought you were saying...... when I begged you be seated......

DR. BLUFF.

I beg your pardon, Prince...... I was not saying anything.

KOURAKIN.

Then I must have been mistaken. [*With an air of extreme indifference.*] How did you like your journey to Russia?

DR. BLUFF.

Very much—very much indeed. Rather fatiguing, though.

KOURAKIN—[*Pointedly.*]

But now that you are in Russia, I hope that you will find your way smoothe and easy..... and..... so far as it may depend on me..... you may be assured that..... For instance, I have discovered that you are not in the good graces of my colleague Nesselrode. He will oppose you near the Emperor. But should Pahlen, who is already devoted to you, I know, be backed by me, you need not care for Nesselrode.

DR. BLUFF.

Indeed! I need not care for Nesselrode! ......

KOURAKIN.

No. But it is on one condition.

DR. BLUFF.

Ho! Ho!

KOURAKIN.

The condition is, that you will use the great and mysterious influence you seem to possess over Pahlen, to make him accept the alliance which is the object of all my wishes. On that condition, I say, I will favor your mission. You see that I come at once to the point, and that I am as plain as you like people to be in America.

DR. BLUFF. [*Aside.*]

You shall have tit for tat. [*To Kourakin.*] So, Sir, whether I deny it or not, you are convinced that I have a diplomatic mission here?

KOURAKIN.

Nesselrode is convinced of it. That is enough for me.

DR. BLUFF.

You are also convinced of my intimate relations with Count Pahlen?

KOURAKIN.

Count Pahlen admits them.

DR. BLUFF.

Well! If he does, I will not contradict him. But let it be understood, that you all assume the responsibility of what may result from those convictions.

KOURAKIN.

Why all these reserves?

DR. BLUFF.

Because I tell you frankly, although you are determined not to believe me, that I don't understand what you are driving at......and therefore I take my precautions, not to be caught in a scrape.

KOURAKIN. [*Aside.*]

What an admirable man! He beats us all at the game we have studied all our lives. It is impossible to find him at fault. [*To Dr. Bluff*] But, Doctor, you would not commit yourself very much by using your influence with Pahlen, to make him favor the alliance......

DR. BLUFF.

Which you have at heart. As to that, sir, I can speak understandingly, for Count Pahlen told me this morning, God only knows why, that he wished me to inform the Emperor, as soon as I got an audience, that he, Count Pahlen, could not gratify your views as to the alliance you speak of. A fact, sir—and it is the only one of which I assume the responsibility.

KOURAKIN.—[*In a passion and rising.*]

Good God! What do I hear! And you make to me this announcement, Sir, in this cool—deliberate manner!

DR. BLUFF. [*Getting excited.*]

In what other way did you expect me to announce it—crying, or laughing?

KOURAKIN.

And it is thus that you dare to lacerate my feelings!

DR. BLUFF.

I am sorry for it—but it is of your own seeking. Everybody, ever since this morning, seems to think that I am a well, out of which something is to be pumped. So, gentle folks, pump—pump—pump away. You will have what you will have.

KOURAKIN.

I see through it all.

DR. BLUFF.

I am glad you do. For I don't.

KOURAKIN.

Sir, such a determination must be due to your influence on Count Pahlen. You must be siding in secret with Nesselrode, and his anger is feigned. Yes—his alliance must have been accepted, and he triumphs over me. [*Fiercely to Dr. Bluff.*] You are at the bottom of all this, Sir.

DR. BLUFF.

At the bottom—or at the top—just as you please. I say—just as you please—for I am determined to let you all have your own way, since I can't comprehend what you are about.

KOURAKIN.

Very well, Sir—continue the part you have assumed. You act it to perfection, I must confess, and I compliment you on your remarkable powers of dissimulation. But I don't choose to dissemble, and I openly tell you that you have in me an enemy whom you will soon find worthy of all your attention. Tremble!—[*Exit in a huff.*]

DR. BLUFF—[*In a towering rage, and shaking his fist at Kourakin.*]

Tremble! Tremble!...... Do you think that you are speaking to one of your serfs! I—Doctor Bluff—a free born American citizen—tremble! Why—man, the word is not in the American vocabulary. [*Snapping his fingers.*] I don't care a pinch of snuff for you all. The broad shield of my country protects me wherever I go. That you will find out.

SCENE V.—ENTER PAHLEN BY A LATERAL DOOR, AND THE VISCOUNTESS BY ONE ON THE OPPOSITE SIDE.

PAHLEN—[*To the Viscountess.*]

How happy I am to meet you! A storm is brewing—our fate is to be decided soon. I have just met Kourakin and Nesselrode—they are both in a rage. [*Seeing Dr. Bluff.*] Ha! Doctor, what have you done?

DR. BLUFF.

What I have done?.....[*Aside.*] Truly—I should like to know what I have been doing ever since this morning, for it seems that I have been moving heaven and earth.

VISCOUNTESS.

What has he done?

PAHLEN.—[*To the Viscountess.*]

Instead of breaking open the matter—first to the Emperor—gradually and with proper caution—he has disclosed it at once to Kourakin and to Nesselrode, who are both in a great state of excitement, and who will prejudice the Emperor against me before I can throw myself at his feet.

VISCOUNTESS.

O heaven! Do you know, Doctor, that the Emperor may declare null and void an engagement that he has not sanctioned—that he may send me back to England—and the Count to Siberia?

PAHLEN.

You ought, my dear Sir, to have felt the ground with the Emperor before making a full disclosure.

DR. BLUFF.

Not at all—not at all. In all difficult cases there is nothing like taking the bull by the horns, as we do in America, in pressing exigencies. It will all come right in the end.—[*Aside.*] I must cheer them up, poor souls; for they look crest-fallen, and it seems that I have involuntarily led them into a scrape.

PAHLEN.

At least, see the Emperor at once.

VISCOUNTESS.

Hasten to show him the earnest appeal to his feelings with which you are intrusted, before Kourakin and Nesselrode have time to urge him to take some harsh decision.

DR. BLUFF—[*Warming up.*]

Yes—I will do it immediately—the more so, that Prince Kourakin has dared to threaten me—me! a free born American citizen! Sacred God! He has told me to tremble! I'll see the Emperor—I'll complain of this outrage—I'll talk plain to the Emperor. I am not the man to be afraid of any Emperor, dead or alive, or of all the Kourakins in the world put together. I am an American citizen—every inch of me, from top to toe.

SCENE VI.—LODOISKA AND THE PRECEDING ACTORS.

LODOISKA—[*Rushing in.*]

O, dear Doctor, how happy I am! Let me shake hands with you. There.......to my heart's content. I am indebted to you for it all. [*The Doctor looks bewildered.*] Yes—it was a master stroke on your part. When I delivered your message to father, and told him that Count Pahlen rejected his alliance, he drew himself up fiercely, and he said: "Well, it seems that Kourakin's alliance is prefered to mine. But to show him my supreme indifference about it, and to convince him that I had at hand a man whom I like just as much as Pahlen, I give you at once to Lipinski." And I say, Doctor, this is all due to you. You are the greatest diplomate in the world.

ALL.

Here is the Emperor!—Here is the Emperor himself!

SCENE VII.—ENTER THE EMPEROR.

EMPEROR.

Doctor Bluff, I wish to speak to you in private. [*To the ladies.*] Your presence is much desired in the dancing room. [*To Pahlen.*] You, Count, repair to my closet, and wait there for my orders.

VISCOUNTESS.

[*In a whisper to Dr. Bluff.*] There comes the crisis. Much depends on you. [*Exit with Lodoiska.*]

PAHLEN.

[*Also in a whisper to the same.*] I should tremble, if I had not faith in your nerves and in your skill. [*Exit.*]

[*The Emperor paces the room in silence, as if communing with himself.*]

DOCTOR BLUFF—[*Aside.*]

Really, I begin to be uneasy—about these people, of course, not about myself. There is no Emperor, or King, or Devil whatever, that an American need fear, as long as he does no harm. He has millions of freemen for his body-guard—ready to avenge his wrongs.

EMPEROR.—[*Stopping short, abruptly.*]

Please to approach, Sir. I have great reproaches to address to you.

DR. BLUFF.

To me? Sire.

EMPEROR.

Your arrival here dates from this morning, and yet, in so short a time, you have greatly contributed to increase the dissensions already existing between my Ministers.

DR. BLUFF.

How can it be possible, Sire......

EMPEROR.

Attempt no defence. I know all. It seems, besides, that on Count Pahlen, with whom you have been long acquainted, you exercise a mysterious influence.

DR. BLUFF.

I swear, Sire......

EMPEROR.

Don't swear. I know all. You have told Kourakin that Pahlen rejects the alliance which the Prince had at heart.

DR. BLUFF.

As to that, Sire, it is true.

EMPEROR.

Good—you admit it. You have dealt in the same way with Nesselrode.

DR. BLUFF.

I confess it.

EMPEROR.

Good—I like your candor. But are you not aware, Sir, that you have consented to be the channel through which the keenest insult has been conveyed to two of my oldest and most faithful servants? Are you not aware that you have, without hesitation, or any scruple whatever, been the cause of planting, perhaps forever, the seeds of discord and reciprocal hostility in the breasts of men whom I love—who are necessary to me—and who, in order the better to serve my interests, ought always to be on the very best terms with each other?

DR. BLUFF.

Sire.........I regret ....

EMPEROR.

Ah! You regret, Sir!..........And what right had you to meddle with affairs which concerned you not? What connection had the alliances you have contributed to break with the mission with which you may have been intrusted? Speak, Sir, speak. What apology have you to offer me, on behalf of Count Pahlen in particular? You ought to know his motives.

DR. BLUFF.

Sire—all that I can comprehend in all this is, that Count Pahlen is in favor of a third alliance, and that he has even contracted engagements to that effect.

EMPEROR.

A third alliance!—Engagements contracted without my consent!...... Without even my knowledge! And it is from you, a perfect stranger here, that I am to learn, for the first time, that a subject thus fails in the respect he owes his sovereign! Wait for me here—Sir. I must to my cabinet, where Count Pahlen expects my orders. [*Exit.*]

DR. BLUFF. [*Alone.*]

Now if a pretty explanation does not come out of all this—why—I am no longer plain Doctor Bluff—and if some evil too comes out of it for some people, whose fault is it?......Not mine, faith! Why did they not explain it all to me from the beginning?

SCENE VIII—ENTER VISCOUNTESS, *precipitately.*

VISCOUNTESS.

Well—what news, Doctor?

DR. BLUFF.

News? Bad. The news is that the Emperor has got his steam up, and is gone to pull the ears of Count Pahlen.

VISCOUNTESS.

Good heavens! Did you tell him all?

DR. BLUFF.

I told him that Count Pahlen had his own notions, and had formed an alliance of his own.

VISCOUNTESS.—[*In great alarm.*]

O! He may be lost! He may be under arrest, he may be on his way to Siberia. I run to throw myself at the feet of the Emperor, and draw all his anger upon me by assuming the whole responsibility of the fault. [*Exit.*]

DR. BLUFF.

Halloo! Things are coming to a conclusion any how. So much the better! I like conclusions. Upon my word this is exciting, and I begin to feel that I am warming into a fever myself.

SCENE IX.

NESSELRODE—[*Hurrying in*]

Doctor, I am content. Glad to tell you so.

DR. BLUFF—[*Aside.*]

Ho! Ho!—Here is a change of tone! What's in the wind now, I wonder?

NESSELRODE.

Yes, Sir—I am well pleased with you. Thanks to your energy, to the promptitude of your decision, and to your manly frankness, everything is arranged. I am just from the Emperor's cabinet, where a full explanation took place, and I repeat it, I am highly pleased with the course pursued by you on this occasion.

DR. BLUFF.

Delighted to hear it...... and thus...... Count Pahlen accepts your alliance?

NESSELRODE.

No!—How can it be? You know better.

DR. BLUFF—[*Perplexed.*]

True—I know better. Then he goes over to Prince Kourakin?......

NESSELRODE.

No! How can you talk so? You know it is impossible.

DR. BLUFF.

True, it is impossible......I had forgotten.

NESSELRODE.

After all—you have succeeded admirably, with all your affectation of ignorance and bluntness. You are an admirable actor—truly a born diplomate.

DR. BLUFF.

Sir, you do me too much honor.

NESSELRODE.

Not at all; for you have pleased everybody—and that is no common secret. As to myself, I am fully satisfied with the arrangement, as it gives Prince Kourakin no advantage over me.

DR. BLUFF.

And Prince Kourakin ?......is he equally .....

NESSELRODE.

Bound to be, my dear Sir—how can it be otherwise ?......From the moment that I got no advantage over him ?......That was all he wanted. That's plain.

DR. BLUFF. [*Aside.*]

Plain to everybody, except to myself.

SCENE X.

PAHLEN—[*Rushing in.*]

Victory ! Doctor, victory ! Thanks to you, all is known—all is explained.

DR. BLUFF.

I am overjoyed to hear it—and so—all is *explained ?* is that a fact ?—a real fact ?

PAHLEN.

To be sure ! How can you doubt it, after what you have done, when you have conducted every thing ?

DR. BLUFF—[*Aside.*]

Heaven be praised ! Now that all is explained, I shall know what I have done.

SCENE XI.—ENTER THE EMPEROR, VISCOUNTESS, LODOISKA, KOURAKIN, LADIES AND GENTLEMEN.

EMPEROR—*To* [*Dr. Bluff.*]

Sir, I avail myself with pleasure of this opportunity of testifying openly my approbation of what you have done. You have shown your horror of concealment and duplicity, and you have acted on behalf of your friend Pahlen, as you would have done for yourself—with manly frankness. That is the proper deportment of a gentleman. It is a lesson which you have given, Sir; and I hope it may profit some of those who hear me. Let them know that, for the future, nothing must be concealed from me. I am above disguise myself—and I want no disguise—in those who ought to have claims to my confidence. [*Whilst saying these words, he looks around the circle of attendants about him.*] I love truth above all. [*To Dr. Bluff.*] Sir, when you return to your country, let it be understood there, that the Emperor of all the Russias loves truth just as much as the President of the United States.

DR. BLUFF.

Sire, these august words shall be repeated. But shall I be permitted to avail myself of this opportunity, when your Majesty seems so well disposed, to present the Resolutions of the "Bluffville Peace Association?" [*Pulls them out of his coat pocket.*]

EMPEROR

Certainly.—[*Takes the paper which he hands over to Nesselrode.*] Have charge of them, Nesselrode, and lay them before me, to-morrow, at the meeting of the Council.

DR. BLUFF.

I hope your Majesty will pardon this interference......

EMPEROR.

Pardon!—Sir. There is no need of pardon, when I am glad of what you call an interference. Peace?—I like the very word! You, in particular, have the right to recommend peace, when you have so powerfully contributed to re-establish concord and harmony around me—among my faithful servants. Nesselrode and Kourakin cannot complain—their dignity cannot be wounded—now that you have boldly come out, and made known at once the previous engagements contracted by Count Pahlen.

DR. BLUFF—[*Aside.*]

I'll have it published in the New York Herald that if the Russian Cabinet is a unit, it is due to Dr. Bluff. The allied powers will be in a rage.

EMPEROR.

And, Sir, I will further add, for your special satisfaction, that I fully ratify the alliance made by Count Pahlen.

DR. BLUFF—[*Aside.*]

Some great alliance that will change the face of the world!...... And I am the cause of it! They will receive me with bonfires, illuminations and processions all over the United States. [*To the Emperor.*] Sire, I will make your magnanimity known from Maine to California.

EMPEROR.

Furthermore, Sir—to give you an additional proof of my satisfaction, I wish you to be the first to know and to inform the President of the United States, that I will sign the treaty in relation to the "Rights of Neutrals," which your Minister plenipotentiary has laid before me.

DR. BLUFF.

Sire, I cannot sufficiently express to your Majesty how grateful I am for so many favors.

EMPEROR.

Nay, Sir—I will do more—to show to the whole world how I appreciate frankness of deportment, plain and honest dealing, and fearless independence, I will cause to be delivered to you, to-morrow, a communication to the President of the United States, containing in the most precise and clearest terms, a full recital of all that you have done here, and I wish it to be recorded as a high testimonial of my esteem for you. [*To the whole company,*] and now let us move on, and join the Empress, who has been somewhat neglected this evening.

[*The Emperor offers his arm to the Viscountess, and the whole train proceeds to the inner appartments.*]

DR. BLUFF—[*Alone.*]

Well—if I am not a great man, who is? Who is to look big, if not plain Dr. Bluff? I have done wonders—that's clear. But what are those wonders? That is the question. It is too late for me to ask any explanation. It would be confessing that I know nothing—that I have done nothing—and that I am nobody. No. No—that won't do, Doctor Bluff. All that remains for me to do, since my friend the Emperor is going to explain it all to my friend the President of the United States, is to start for home to-morrow, and learn at Washington what I have been doing at St. Petersburg

THE END.

The author acknowledges with pleasure that he is indebted for some of his inspirations to Scribe's Vaudeville: *Le Diplomate.*